the DINOSAUR FUN BOOK

By Gillian Osband
Illustrated by Jonathan Allen

ISBN 0-590-43734-8

First published by Scholastic Ltd., 1986. Copyright © 1984 Manor Lodge Productions Limited, 1986. All rights reserved. Published by Scholastic Inc.

12 11 10 9 8 7 6 5 4 3 2 1   9/8 0 1 2 3/9

Printed in the U.S.A.   08

First Scholastic printing, April 1987

SCHOLASTIC INC.
New York Toronto London Auckland Sydney

WHAT'S INSIDE. . . . .

	Page
FUN WITH DINOSAURS	3
Dinosaur Groups	3
TYRANNOSAURUS BOWLING	4–5
PUZZLE FUN	6–7
DOUGHY DINOSAURS	8–9
HOW TO DRAW YOUR	
FAVORITE DINOSAURS	10–11
DELICIOUS DINOSAURS!	12–13
CHRISTMAS CREATURES	14–15
DANGER DINOSAURS! An	
Exciting Prehistoric Board	
Game	16–17
DINOSAUR DOMINOES	18–19
YOUR DINOSAUR SCRAPBOOK	20–21
DINOSAURS FROM BITS AND	
PIECES	22–23
FINGER, THUMB AND HAND	
DINOSAURS	24–25
ARCHAEOPTERYX KITE	26–28
DOTTY DINOSAUR	29
EGGOSAURUS!	30–31

READ THESE TIPS FIRST

Before you start to make anything in this book, read the instructions and gather together all the things you need.

If there is anything you don't understand – or if you are stuck – **ASK AN ADULT FOR HELP.**

How To Trace:

If you need to cut something out of paper: You should be able to put the paper over the drawing and trace right onto the paper. The paper should be thin enough for you to see through.

If you want to cut something out of cardboard, dough or material: Use tracing paper to trace the drawing. Cut it out. Put the pattern on the cardboard/dough, etc. Draw around it with a pencil and cut it out – or you may be able to cut around your pattern with a **blunt** knife or scissors. **With material:** Pin your pattern to it.

FUN WITH DINOSAURS

The word **DINOSAUR** means "Terrible Lizard." Not all dinosaurs were terrible – and **NONE** of them was a lizard! All dinosaurs were **REPTILES** – but not **ALL** reptiles were dinosaurs!

The early dinosaurs were small creatures. **Coelophysis,** one of the first dinosaurs, was about 3 feet high and only 8–10 feet long and half of that was tail. **Tyrannosaurus Rex,** one of the last dinosaurs, was more than 40 feet long, 16 feet high and weighed more than 8 tons – that's bigger than a bus!

Dinosaurs ruled the Earth for 140 million years – 70 times as long as MAN has existed!

DINOSAUR GROUPS

Dinosaurs are divided into these groups:

ORNITHISCHIANS
– Their hip–bones were arranged like this:

They are called "bird–hipped."

1. **Ornithopods:** e.g., **Iguanodon;** usually walked on 2 legs.

2. **Ankylosaurs:** e.g., **Nodosaurus;** 4–footed with short legs and heavy bodies; protected with body armor; tails often with spikes or clubs at the end.

3. **Ceratopsians:** e.g., **Triceratops;** usually 4–footed; all had large, well–protected heads, often with fierce horns.

4. **Stegosaurs:** e.g., **Stegosaurus;** 4–footed; the front legs usually shorter than the back; protected by armor plating and often spikes too.

SAURISCHIANS
– Their hip–bones were arranged like this:

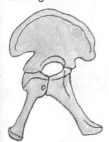

They are called "lizard–hipped."

1. **Sauropods:** e.g., **Brachiosaurus;** gigantic, with huge bodies and bones; walked on 4 legs; small heads; long necks; "gentle giants."

2. **Therapods**
    a) **Carnosaurs:** e.g., **Tyrannosaurus Rex;** big dinosaurs; big heads and huge bones; short necks; large hind legs and short front ones; all fierce, meat–eating hunters.

    b) **Coelurosaurs:**
    e.g., **Compsognathus;** small; birdlike; with long necks and small heads; hollow bones.

TYRANNOSAURUS BOWLING

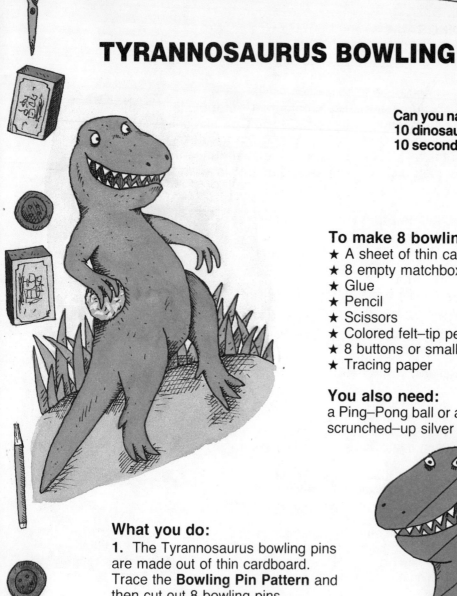

Can you name 10 dinosaurs in 10 seconds?

Nine Protoceratops and a Diplodocus.

To make 8 bowling pins you need:
★ A sheet of thin cardboard
★ 8 empty matchboxes
★ Glue
★ Pencil
★ Scissors
★ Colored felt–tip pens or paints
★ 8 buttons or small pebbles
★ Tracing paper

You also need:
a Ping–Pong ball or a ball made from scrunched–up silver foil.

Bowling Pin Pattern

What you do:
1. The Tyrannosaurus bowling pins are made out of thin cardboard. Trace the **Bowling Pin Pattern** and then cut out 8 bowling pins.

(Look at page 2 for **Tracing Instructions**.)

2. With a black felt–tip pen draw the face, claws and tail on each bowling pin.

3. Number your bowling pins from **1–8**.

4. With your pens or paints make each Tyrannosaurus as bright as you can.

5. Put a button or pebble in each matchbox to act as a weight.

6. On the back and at the bottom of each Tyrannosaurus, glue a matchbox. Your bowling pin will now stand up.

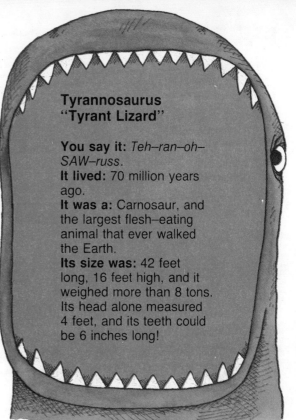

Tyrannosaurus "Tyrant Lizard"

You say it: *Teh–ran–oh–SAW–russ.*
It lived: 70 million years ago.
It was a: Carnosaur, and the largest flesh–eating animal that ever walked the Earth.
Its size was: 42 feet long, 16 feet high, and it weighed more than 8 tons. Its head alone measured 4 feet, and its teeth could be 6 inches long!

7. Stand your bowling pins in a group on the floor or on a table top. Roll your ball at them from about 4 feet away.

8. Take turns rolling the ball. Add up the numbers on the bowling pins you have knocked over. Try to hit the high numbers. Whoever gets a score of 40 first is the winner.

PUZZLE FUN

DOPEY DINOSAURS

If you can help this Cetiosaurus find its way through the **JUNGLE MAZE** to the swamp you will save him from the ferocious **SPINOSAURUS** who wants him for his dinner.

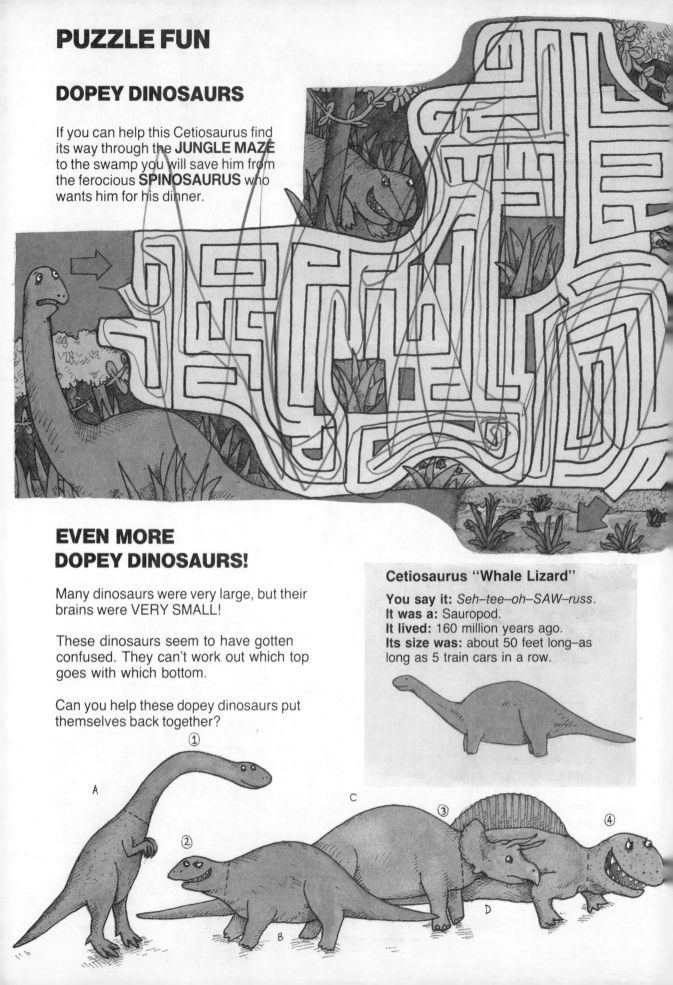

EVEN MORE DOPEY DINOSAURS!

Many dinosaurs were very large, but their brains were VERY SMALL!

These dinosaurs seem to have gotten confused. They can't work out which top goes with which bottom.

Can you help these dopey dinosaurs put themselves back together?

Cetiosaurus "Whale Lizard"

You say it: *Seh–tee–oh–SAW–russ*.
It was a: Sauropod.
It lived: 160 million years ago.
Its size was: about 50 feet long–as long as 5 train cars in a row.

COLORFUL CREATURES

Here are some dinosaurs to color.

Their names mean:
"Bird Stealer"
"Many–spined"
"Thick–nosed Lizard"

. . .but these meanings are not in the right order.
Can you fit the correct meaning to each dinosaur's name?

Remember: You can use these shapes to make some of the things in the rest of the book.

AN APA–DIP – GORG–SAURUS . . . A WHAT?

YOU can invent a **new** dinosaur!

You need:
Paper
crayons
2 or more players.

How to play:
1. The first player draws a dinosaur head — and then folds the paper leaving just a tiny bit of drawing showing.

2. The next player draws the next part of the body (**without seeing the head**) — and folds the paper to cover most of the drawing.

3. Each player does this until the dinosaur is complete. The last player has to invent a new name for this prehistoric monster.

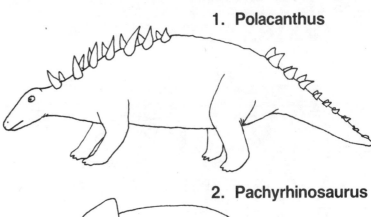

1. Polacanthus

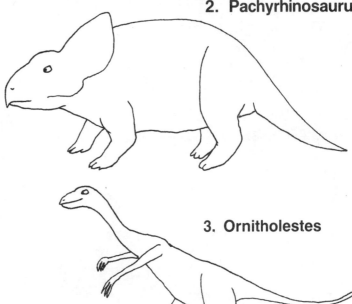

2. Pachyrhinosaurus

3. Ornitholestes

Jungle Maze Solution

DOUGHY DINOSAURS

To make about 8 DOUGHY DINOSAURS you need:

* ★ 1¼ cups salt
* ★ 5 cups plain flour
* ★ 1¼ cups water
* ★ Paper ★ Pencil
* ★ Scissors
* ★ Baking tray
* ★ Poster paints

* ★ Tracing paper
* ★ Egg white to varnish
* ★ Cooking oil
* ★ Glue ★ Tape
* ★ Ribbon
* ★ Safety pins

With **BREAD DOUGH** you can make:

★ **BADGES** ★ **PENDANTS** ★ **UNUSUAL CHRISTMAS TREE DECORATIONS** ★ **PAPER WEIGHTS** . . . AND MUCH, MUCH MORE!

What you do:

1. Mix the flour and salt and water together until you have a stiff dough. Use your fingers to knead it well so that it doesn't crack when you bake it.

2. **For decorations and pendants:** Roll the dough out flat with a rolling pin so that it is about ¼ of an inch thick.

Trace some of the **Dinosaur Patterns** on the next page.

Cut them out; lay them on the dough and cut the dough along the pattern with a **blunt** knife. Make a small hole in the top with a pencil (for the thread to go through).

3. **For badges:** do the same as with the decorations, but do NOT make a hole.

4. **For paperweights and table decorations:** Knead the dough and model it like clay. If you make the model out of several pieces you may need to dampen the ends to make them stick together.

5. Rub the oil over the baking tray to grease it. **Ask an adult to turn on the oven.** Bake for 2½–3 hours at 250°F.

6. When cool, paint your dinosaurs with bright colors. When the paint is dry, paint them with egg white to varnish them.

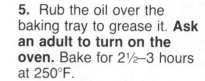
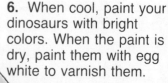
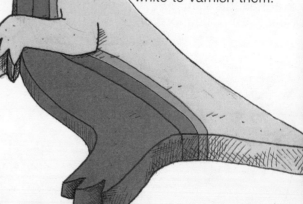

To finish:

7. Thread ribbon through the hole for tree decorations, pendant or mobile.

For the badge, glue a safety pin on the back, and then put a piece of tape across the pin to make it secure.

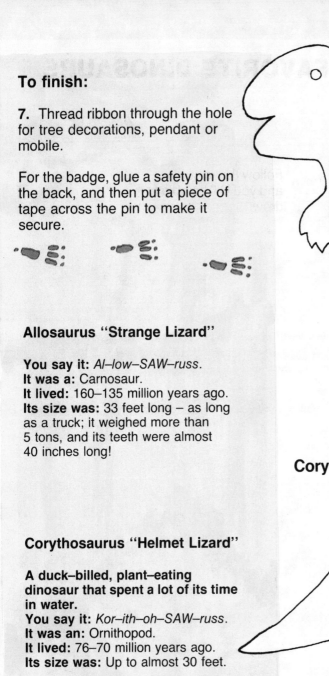

Allosaurus "Strange Lizard"

You say it: *Al–low–SAW–russ*.
It was a: Carnosaur.
It lived: 160–135 million years ago.
Its size was: 33 feet long – as long as a truck; it weighed more than 5 tons, and its teeth were almost 40 inches long!

Corythosaurus "Helmet Lizard"

A duck–billed, plant–eating dinosaur that spent a lot of its time in water.
You say it: *Kor–ith–oh–SAW–russ*.
It was an: Ornithopod.
It lived: 76–70 million years ago.
Its size was: Up to almost 30 feet.

Brachiosaurus "Arm Lizard"

It had the biggest body and the smallest brain!
You say it: *Brack–ee–oh–SAW–russ*.
It was a: Sauropod.
It lived: 160–135 million years ago.
Its size was: 75 feet long; tallest known dinosaur; it weighed more than 80 tons!

Patterns

How can you tell if a dinosaur's been in the fridge?

Huge claw marks in the butter.

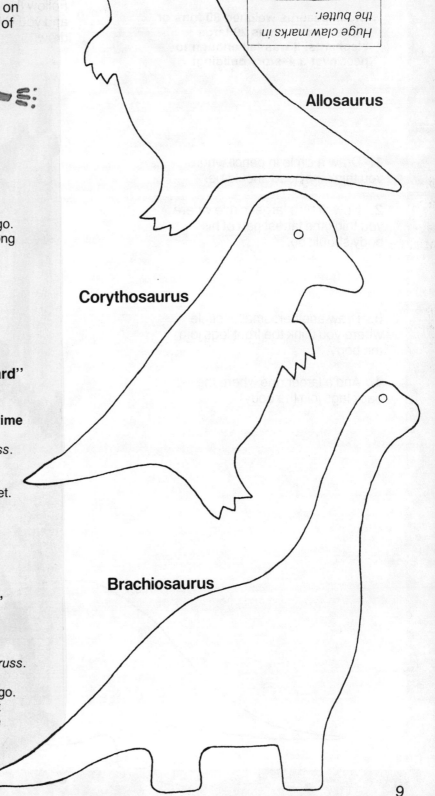

Allosaurus

Corythosaurus

Brachiosaurus

HOW TO DRAW YOUR FAVORITE DINOSAURS

Brachiosaurus "Arm Lizard"

Brachiosaurus weighed 80 tons or more – as much as 20 large elephants! It was tall enough to peer over a 4–story building!

Follow these steps and you will be able to draw. . .

1. Draw a circle in pencil where you think the head should be.

2. Now draw a larger circle where you think the fattest part of his body should be.

3. Draw another, smaller circle where you think the front legs join the body.

4. And a larger one where the back legs join the body.

Brachiosaurus

Tyrannosaurus Rex "Tyrant Lizard"

He was as tall as a giraffe. He was as long as two giraffes lying down. He was as heavy as 1½ elephants. He mainly ate other dinosaurs.

5. Draw even smaller circles where the nose is and where the knees are. For the tail, draw lots of circles getting smaller and smaller.

Tyrannosaurus Rex

Spinosaurus "Spine Lizard"

A savage meat–eating dinosaur.
You say it: *Spy–no–SAW–russ*.
It was a: Carnosaur.
It lived: 130–100 million years ago.
Its size was: about 35 feet long; the spines on its back were about 6½ feet long!

6. Now with a pen, draw the outline of your dinosaur (you can do it first in pencil and then draw over it), joining the circles with curved lines, as you can see in the pictures. When the ink is dry, erase the pencil circles.

Spinosaurus

You can now draw any dinosaur you like. You can even invent some of your own!

DELICIOUS DINOSAURS!

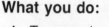

Scrumptious Shortbread

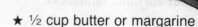

For about 20 cookies you need:

★ ½ cup butter or margarine
★ ¼ cup granulated sugar
★ 1 cup plain flour
★ 20 raisins or currants
★ Cooking oil
★ ¼ cup almonds
★ Whisk ★ Knife ★ Bowl
★ Baking tray
★ Rolling pin
★ Clean surface
★ Paper ★ Pencil
★ Scissors

What you do:

1. Trace and cut out the **cookie patterns.**

2. Ask an adult to turn on the oven to 350°F.

3. Beat the sugar and butter in the bowl until they are well mixed and creamy. (If your mother has an electric mixer, she may cream them for you.)

4. Add the flour, a little at a time, and knead it with your hand into the mixture.

5. Use paper towels to rub the cooking oil over the baking tray to grease it.

6. When the dough is well mixed, sprinkle some flour on a clean surface (or a pastry board). Roll out your dough.

Roll a bit, then turn it over and roll some more. If it begins to stick to the rolling pin or board, sprinkle some more flour on both sides.

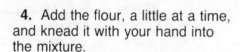

7. When the dough is about ¼ of an inch thick, lay the cookie patterns on the dough. Cut around them with a **blunt** knife.

Put the cookies on a baking tray. Cut out as many cookies as you can. Then knead all the leftover dough together. Roll it out again until you have cut as many cookies as you can.

8. Use a raisin for each eye. Draw a mouth with the knife. Break the nuts in half. Stick them into the Nodosaurus to make its knobs and spikes.

9. Prick each cookie twice with the prongs of a fork.

10. Put the baking tray in the middle of the oven. Let the cookies bake for about 20 minutes. Then look at them. If they are pale brown and crisp, they are ready. If not, leave them in for another 5 minutes.

11. When ready, take them out of the oven. Turn the oven off. Sprinkle with sugar and let them cool. Lift your cookies off the tray with a wide knife.

Apatosaurus "Unreal Lizard"

A gentle plant–eating giant.
You say it: *Ah–pat–oh–SAW–russ*.
It was a: Sauropod.
It lived: 190 million years ago.
Its size was: more than 65 feet long; and it weighed over 30 tons.

Cookie Patterns

ALWAYS USE POT HOLDERS TO LIFT HOT THINGS.

REMEMBER: OVENS ARE HOT. ALWAYS ASK AN ADULT FOR HELP.

Nodosaurus "Knobbed Lizard"

You say it: *Node–oh–SAW–russ*.
It was an: Ankylosaur.
It lived: 70–100 million years ago.
Its size was: more than 14 feet long.

TURN THE OVEN OFF WHEN YOU HAVE FINISHED.

Scrumposaurus!!!!!

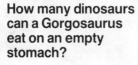

How many dinosaurs can a Gorgosaurus eat on an empty stomach?

One – after that it's stomach won't be empty!

Why does a Spinosaurus eat raw meat?

Because he doesn't know how to cook.

CHRISTMAS CREATURES

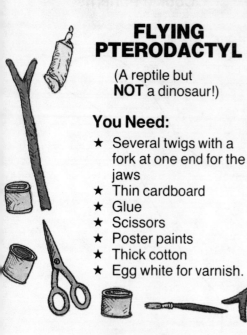

FLYING PTERODACTYL

(A reptile but **NOT** a dinosaur!)

You Need:

★ Several twigs with a fork at one end for the jaws
★ Thin cardboard
★ Glue
★ Scissors
★ Poster paints
★ Thick cotton
★ Egg white for varnish.

What you do:

1. Break off any bits along the length of the twig.

2. The size of the teeth, back legs and wings depends on the size of each twig, and on the size of the forked end.

3. Cut a strip off one end of the cardboard. Draw the teeth like this:

Cut the teeth out. Glue them along the two forked pieces like this:

Draw two back legs like this:

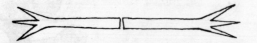

4. Cut the legs out and paint them green. When they are dry, glue them to the back of the twig like this:

5. Fold the rest of the cardboard in half. Draw the wing shape on it. Then draw the "arms" and claws.

6. Cut around the outside edge. Paint the "arms" the same color as the legs.

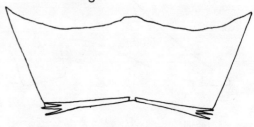

Paint both sides of the wings.

Pterodactyls were probably grayish–green in color, but no one really knows. So why don't you paint yours in bright colors?

7. Paint the "body" – the twig. Again use bright colors.

8. When the twig and wings are dry, glue the wings around the stick, like this:

9. Make two small holes near the top of the wings. Thread the cotton through the holes, knot it at the top, and hang it on the tree.

If you paint your Pterodactyls in different colors, they will make extraordinary **CHRISTMAS CREATURES!**

Pterodactyl "Wing Finger"

You say it: *TEHR–o–DAK–til*.
It lived: about 190 million years ago.
It was a: Pterosaur, a flying reptile that ate insects and fish.
Its size was: about 40 inches across its open wings.

A Pterodactyl's two front limbs were covered with skin to form wings. The first 3 "fingers" were its claws, and the 4th was very long so it could support the wing skin.

What's the difference between a dinosaur and a banana?

A banana's yellow.

15

DANGER DINOSAURS

To make your markers:

Trace these markers onto thin cardboard. Color them. Cut them out. Cut up the middle of the bottom. Bend one half of the bottom back, and the other half forward, so your marker stands up.

To make your dice:

Knead a piece of modeling clay into a square and mark the numbers with a pencil point . . . or make a **bread dough** dice (see p. 8). The **dice pattern** shows you how to mark your dice. (You can also use a ready-made dice from another game.)

RULES

The first person to throw a 6 starts. Take turns throwing the dice and moving your dinosaur the right number of places. If you land on a square where a shortcut starts, go down it.

The winner is the one who reaches the cave first. You must throw the correct number to go into it. If you throw a higher number, you have to go back down the board again.

To make the game more difficult. . . .

Cut out about 20 pieces of paper the size of a playing card. On each write – a challenge, or a dinosaur question and answer; a dinosaur riddle; how to spell different dinosaurs; ask the player to make up a dinosaur story or rhyme.

If a player lands on a number ending with a 3 or 5, the player on the right picks up a card – and reads what's on it. If the player can't do what's on the card, he misses a turn.

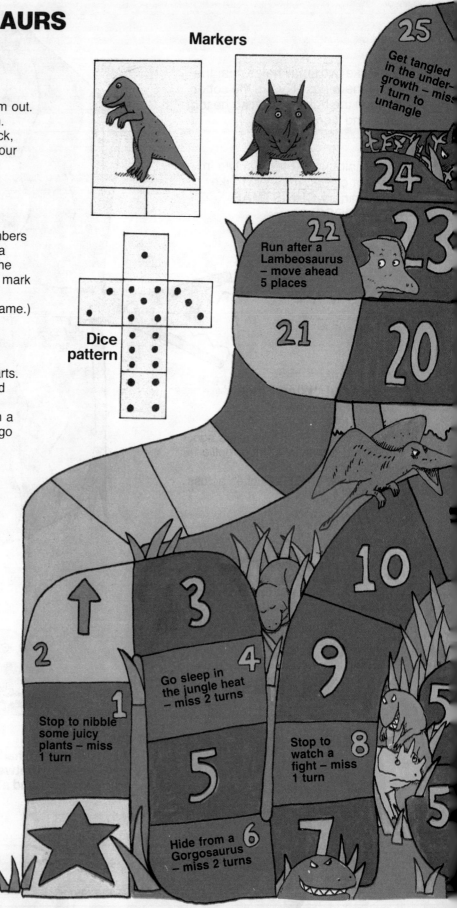

Markers

Dice pattern

25 Get tangled in the under-growth – miss 1 turn to untangle

24

23

22 Run after a Lambeosaurus – move ahead 5 places

21

20

10

9

8 Stop to watch a fight – miss 1 turn

7

6 Hide from a Gorgosaurus – miss 2 turns

5

4 Go sleep in the jungle heat – miss 2 turns

3

2

1 Stop to nibble some juicy plants – miss 1 turn

DINOSAUR DOMINOES

You need:
- ★ Large sheet of thin cardboard
- ★ 1 empty matchbox
- ★ Scissors
- ★ Ruler
- ★ Pencil
- ★ Paints or colored felt–tip pens

To make your dominoes:

1. Put the matchbox on the cardboard and draw around it. Do this another 27 times.

2. Divide each box you have drawn in half. Choose 7 different dinosaurs and draw your set of dinosaur dominoes like this:

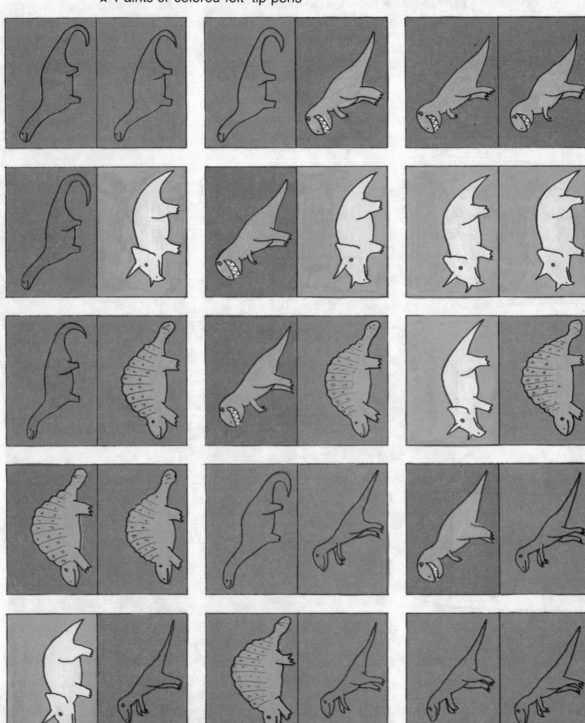

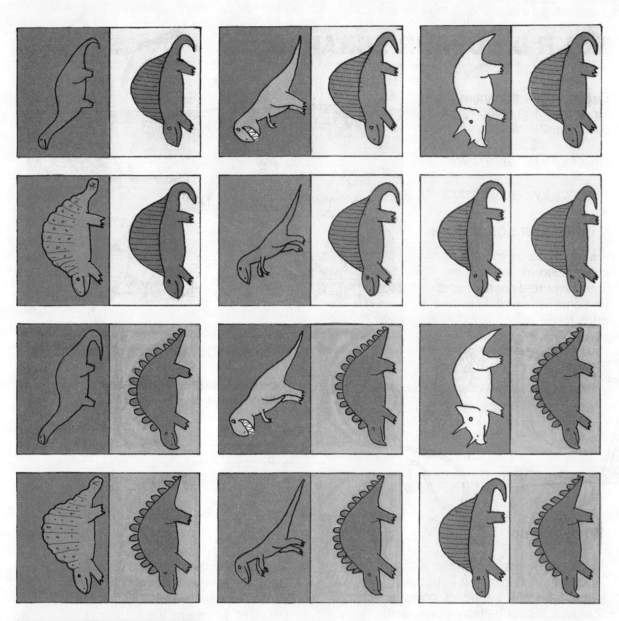

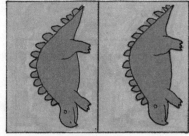

3. Cut them out. Now you are ready to play.

How to play:

1. Give each player an equal amount of dominoes. Don't let anyone else see your pictures. Place any extra dominoes face down in a central pile.

2. One player starts by putting a domino, showing the pictures, on the table.

3. The next player adds a matching domino. If he hasn't got one, he can take an extra domino from the central pile – and misses a turn.

4. Players take turns adding matching dinosaurs.

Use the dominoes from the central pile until they are all used up. When they are all gone, a player who can't add to the row misses a turn.

5. The first person to add all his dominoes to the row is the winner.

There are many games you can play with dominoes. Borrow a book from the library to find out what they are.

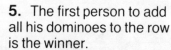

Which dinosaurs eat with their tails?

They all do – none of them can take their tails off when they eat!

YOUR DINOSAUR SCRAPBOOK

Did you know that there are more than 100 different dinosaurs?

How many do you know?

Why don't you make yourself a . . .

DINOSAUR SCRAPBOOK

– and collect as much information as you can on your favorite dinosaurs and on some less well–known ones too?

To make your scrapbook you need:

★ Several large sheets of paper – the same size – they can be different colors
★ Scissors
★ Ribbon
★ Pencil
★ Reinforcements (if possible)

What you do:

1. Put 5 sheets of paper in a pile. About an inch from the left edge, press hard with the pencil point in 2 places, about halfway down, like this:

The mark will show through to all the sheets, and this is where you make your holes so that they are all in the same place. Use the end of the scissors to make a small hole at each mark.

2. Take another 5 sheets. On the top of the pile put a sheet with holes. Press through the holes with your pencil so you make the marks in the right place.

3. When you have made holes in all the sheets, stick a reinforcement over each hole so that the paper doesn't tear.

4. Thread the ribbon through the two holes and tie it in a bow.

Don't tie the bow too tightly otherwise you won't be able to turn the pages. You can add new sheets by undoing the ribbon.

Ideas for your scrapbook:

★ All the facts you can find
★ Any extraordinary features
★ Your own drawings
★ Postcards
★ Newspaper cuttings
★ Poems, riddles, jokes
★ Stories

Make each page as colorful and as interesting as you can.

Here are some dinosaurs you may not have heard of before:

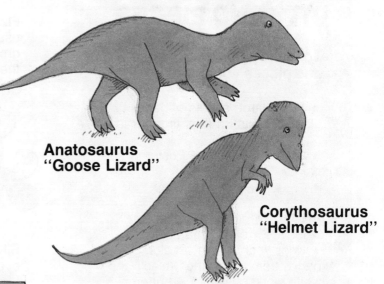

Anatosaurus
"Goose Lizard"

Corythosaurus
"Helmet Lizard"

Ornitholestes
"Bird Stealer"

Dilophosaurus
"Two–ridged Lizard"

What is almost 50 feet high, weighs more than 80 tons and is noisy?

A Brachiosaurus with a set of drums!

IT'S AMAZING!

Protoceratops is a very common dinosaur. What is unusual is that eggs, newly–hatched babies, half–grown and fully–grown adults have all been found.

DINOSAURS FROM BITS AND PIECES

To make pictures from bits and pieces you need:

★ Some large sheets of paper to glue your bits on (the stronger the paper the better)
★ Glue ★ Scissors ★ Poster paints

AND . . . ★ pebbles ★ shells ★ leaves ★ bits of material ★ twigs ★ dry pasta ★ color pages from magazines (black and white works well too) ★ buttons ★ cork ★ metal bottle tops ★ silver foil ★ feathers ★ tissue paper – and anything else you think might work for your pictures.

TIP: Keep a box for bits and pieces so that you always have a good collection of things to use. Keep each type of thing in a separate bag or smaller box – and if you can't see what it contains, label it.

When you make a picture out of bits and pieces you can decide to use only one or two types of bits – or you can use a whole mixture of things.

Think about what you want in your picture – and then decide which bits and pieces will work best. Draw the outlines before you begin.

Glue all your bits and pieces in place and press them onto the paper. Make sure everything is dry before you move it. You can also paint shells, pasta and pebbles whatever color you need them to be.

Here are some suggestions:

Flat pebbles and shells: are useful for mountains and the ground. Also, for spiky parts of the dinosaur's body.

Silver foil: good for teeth, claws, eyes and pools of water.

Shaped pasta and pasta shells: make flowers and tree trunks.

Straight pasta bits: make dinosaur spikes. Paint them green for grass.

Cork: is good for tree trunks, dinosaur horns and the ground.

Scrunched up tissue paper: use for tree tops, flowers and insects.

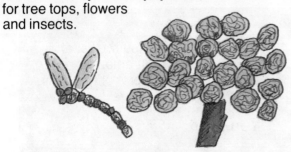

Bits of material: cut them into small pieces and glue them in patchwork bits to make flowers, dinosaurs' bodies, trees etc.

Twigs: use for trees. Make some dinosaurs' legs from straight bits.

Leaves: good for dinosaurs' bodies, flowers and treetops.

Beads: make eyes and the centers of flowers.

Metal bottle tops: use for armor plating and spikes.

Feathers: good for jungle fronds. You can dip them in paint and press them on the paper to make a frond print.

LEAF

BEADS

BALLS OF TISSUE PAPER

BLUE MATERIAL

FOIL

HALF A LEAF

PINK MATERIAL

CORDUROY

PASTA

SPAGHETTI

TWIG

FOIL

CORK

STONES

VARIOUS MATERIAL

FINGER, THUMB AND HAND DINOSAURS

Using your finger, thumb, fist and hand, you can print amazing dinosaurs . . . and probably messy ones too!

You need:

★ Poster paints
★ Water
★ Several saucers or tin–foil containers
★ Paper for your pictures
★ Lots of newspaper
★ A rag
★ Your hand. . . .

TIP:

Don't put too much water with your paint. It needs to be "sticky" to give a good print.

TIP:

Dab your fingertip into the paint, and then press gently onto the paper.

You will know if the paint stickiness is right if you can see the swirls and lines of your fingertips.

What you do:

1. Spread lots of newspaper around where you are painting.

2. Put a different–colored paint in each saucer. Keep a couple of saucers for mixing colors.

3. **Before you start your picture:** Dip your thumb, finger–tips, palm of your hand, your fist, the side of your hand, your little finger in the paint and see what shapes they make. Try rolling them on the paper too.

See if you can copy this picture.
Then try some of your own.

You can either make your whole picture from your prints, or you can stick bits and pieces on to make the background. You can also paint in details like the eyes and mouth.

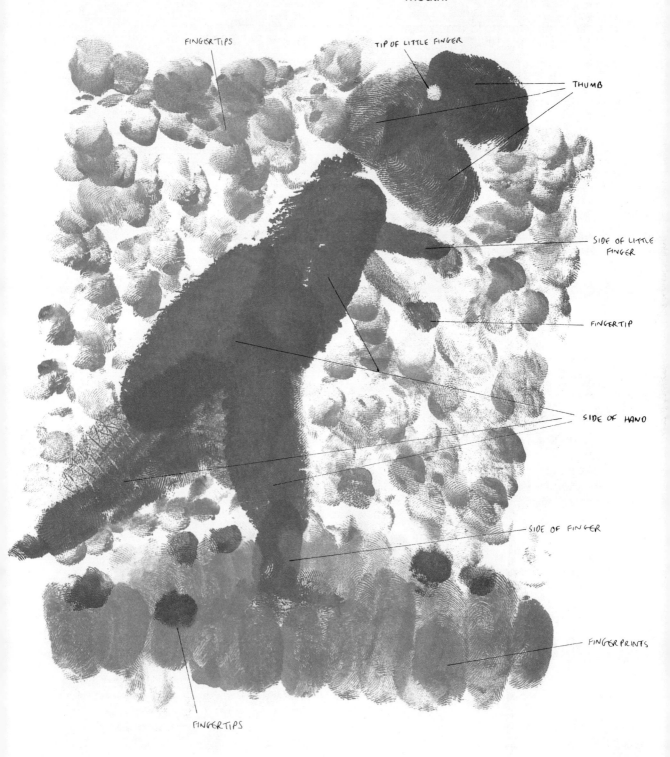

FINGERTIPS

TIP OF LITTLE FINGER

THUMB

SIDE OF LITTLE FINGER

FINGERTIP

SIDE OF HAND

SIDE OF FINGER

FINGER PRINTS

FINGERTIPS

ARCHAEOPTERYX KITE

This is a **CHEAT! WHY?** Because Archaeopteryx was **NOT** a dinosaur – but he **IS** thought to have been the **FIRST BIRD.**

Before you start **READ THESE INSTRUCTIONS CAREFULLY.** If you get stuck **ASK FOR HELP.**

You may need some help measuring out your kite. The important thing is to get the **shape.**

If you want a smaller kite, measure the places where the support sticks need to go. Then cut the support strips to fit. Remember to make the longer strip overlap the top of the kite by 2 inches.

What you do:

1. With the ruler and felt–tip pen measure out the pattern in **Drawing 1.** Draw the lines and then cut out your kite along the **solid** lines. Do **NOT** cut along the dotted lines.

You need:

* ★ A piece of plain–colored paper at least 24 inches wide and 27 inches long
* ★ Tape ★ Scissors ★ Glue ★ Ruler
* ★ 2 strips of thick cardboard 17½ inches long
* ★ 1 strip of thick cardboard 25½ inches long
* ★ Large ball of string
* ★ Paper napkins for the tail
* ★ Colored felt–tip pens or paints
* ★ Thin cardboard at least 10 inches long and 4 inches wide

6 inches · 6 inches
10½ inches · 10½ inches
17½ inches · 17½ inches · 17½ inches
20½ inches · 20½ inches
6 inches

1.

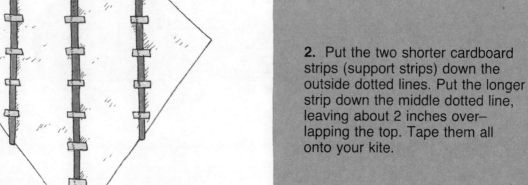

2. Put the two shorter cardboard strips (support strips) down the outside dotted lines. Put the longer strip down the middle dotted line, leaving about 2 inches over–lapping the top. Tape them all onto your kite.

3. Cut out the air vent. With your scissors, make two holes for the string at both corners of the wings (not too near the edge) and one at the base of the tail. Stick a reinforcement over each hole.

4. To make the head:

Fold the thin cardboard in half, lengthwise. Draw the Archaeopteryx's head, with the back of the head along the fold. Cut it out – do **NOT** cut along the fold. Draw on the eyes, and paint the head.

5. To make the body:

Turn the kite over. Copy the Archaeopteryx's body and color it in.

Glue the head around the overlapping stick at the top, facing forward.

6. To make the tail:

Cut a piece of string, about 80 inches long. Cut out 18 "feathers" about 2 inches wide and 6 inches long from the paper napkins. Glue them, at regular intervals, along the tail string. Tie one end of the string through the tail hole, and knot it.

7. Cut another piece of string about 30 inches long. Tie each end through a wing hole.

Attach your flying string to the middle of the string tied to the wings. Make sure it is firmly attached – you don't want your kite to fly off!

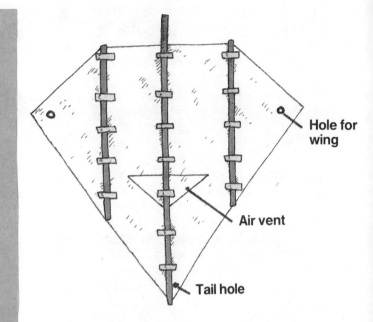

Hole for wing

Air vent

Tail hole

4.

5.

"Feather" for tail

Flying string

6.

7.

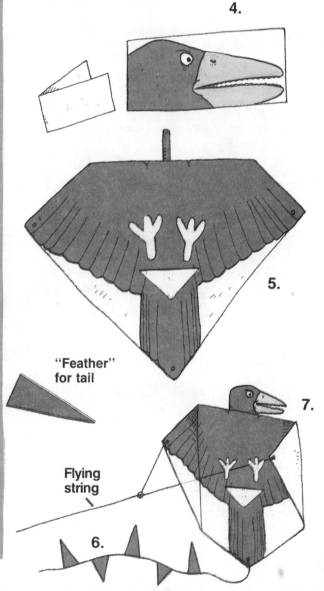

27

How to fly an Archaeopteryx

★Never fly your kite near electrical wires.

★Stay away from trees. You don't want your Archaeopteryx to land in the branches — and stay there!

★Try and fly your kite on rolling hills or flat ground. You do need some wind, but not a gale!

★**How to launch your kite:** stand with your back to the wind. Hold the kite up to the wind with one hand and hold the flying line with the other. As the kite rises, let the line tug gently through your fingers.

★Pull the kite evenly towards you if your kite drops.

★Never run with your kite.

★If you let the line run away through your fingers, the kite will fall away from you and sink. Walk away from it, pulling the line in as you do so.

★If it becomes skittish, walk slowly towards it, letting the line out slowly.

★The tail balances your kite. You will have to experiment with the number of feathers on the tail. You may need more – or you may have too many.

Archaeopteryx "Ancient Wing"

You say it: *AR–kee–OP–ter–ix.*
It lived: about 200 million years ago.
Its size was: similar to a pigeon.

IT'S AMAZING

The most famous and valuable fossil in the world is the Archaeopteryx at the National History Museum, London. It is worth more than $3.5 million.

DOTTY DINOSAUR

Join the dots to find out what this **DOTTY DINOSAUR** is doing – then color it in.

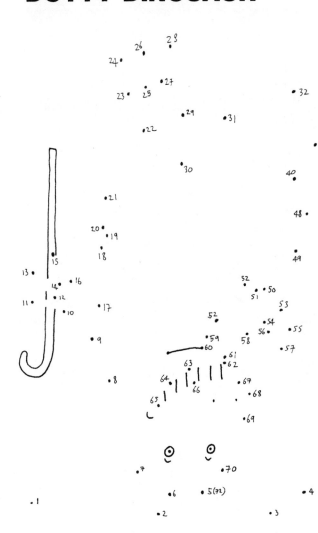

IT'S AMAZING

In 1877, miners in Bernis–sart, Belgium, found they were tunneling through a mass of huge skeletons. They were 975 feet below ground – and the bones were Iguanodon skele–tons!

We know what some duck-billed dinosaurs ate. Some fossils were found and the contents of their stomachs were so well preserved that you could see pine needles, seeds, fruits and twigs.

IT'S AMAZING

The smallest dinosaur found is Compsog–nathus. It was only about 12 inches long – yet it looked like a tiny version of its huge flesh–eating cousins!

If you were walking in the jungle and saw a Tyrannosaurus waking up from his nap, what time would it be?

Time to run!

IT'S AMAZING

Stegosaurus was over 20 feet long, as long as 5 children with their arms outstretched. It weighed more than 2 tons – and had a brain no bigger than a walnut!

EGGOSAURUS!

To make dinosaurs from eggs you must first **BLOW AN EGG** like this:

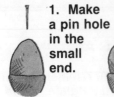

1. Make a pin hole in the small end.

2. Make a pin hole in the large end.

3. Make the second hole bigger with scissors.

4. Break the yolk with the pin.

5. Shake the egg.

6. Blow egg out of its shell into a bowl.

7. Rinse the egg shell and let it dry.

Paint your **EGGOSAURUSES** in bright colors.

To make these Eggosauruses you need:

★ 1 blown egg for each one
★ Thin cardboard
★ White paper
★ Tracing paper
★ Egg carton (cardboard one if possible)
★ Scissors
★ Tape
★ Glue
★ Poster paints
★ Modeling clay

Paleoscincus "Ancient Kind of Lizard"

A plant–eater that had armor plating and spikes to protect it from the fierce meat–eaters.

You say it: *Pal–ee–oh–SKINK–USS.*
It was an: Ankylosaur.
It lived: 80–70 million years ago.
Its size was: 15 feet long, and it weighed more than 4 tons.

1. Trace the head and tail onto the paper. Cut them out. Draw 16 spikes and cut them out.

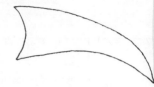

2. The legs are made from cardboard. Trace these patterns and cut them out.

3. Paint the egg. Make the armor plating out of bits of modeling clay and stick them along the top. You can paint the armor plating along the top if you prefer.

4. Paint the head, tail, legs and spikes. When they are dry, glue them to the egg body.

Triceratops "Three–horned Lizard"

A plant–eater about the size of an elephant. Its great enemy was Tyrannosaurus Rex, and it protected itself with its horns and great collar of bone at the back of its neck.

1. Trace the 4 legs. Cut them out of cardboard.

Trace the tail onto paper. Cut it out.

2. To make the head:

Cut a cone from the egg carton.

Cut another cone, but **DON'T** trim the top. Then cut the bottom of the cone off – to leave a "collar."

You say it: *Try–SERR–uh–tops*.
It was a: Ceratopsid.
It lived: 70 million years ago.
Its size was: over 20 feet long; it weighed more than 7–8 tons.

Cut 2 long horns and one short one from the cardboard.

You can either glue them on – or make tiny slits with the end of your scissors and push them through.

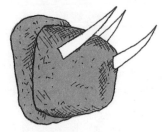

Glue the first cone into the "horned collar."

3. Paint the legs, tail, head and egg body. When they are all dry, glue your Triceratops together.

TIP: You may prefer to stick the legs and tail on the egg with clear tape.

Why did the dinosaur cross the road?

Because there weren't any chickens in those days.